I Made a New Friend Today

By Jason Valenstein and
Margaret Valenstein

Little Stoics Children's Books - Volume 3

For Hilary & Henry

-JV & MV

Reading Note:

The big picture often eludes us, especially when something is at stake, no matter how minor.

Over time children learn to stop focusing on the wrong things, the small things, and increasingly identify and act on opportunities to positively contribute to their peer communities.

It's the author's hope that this real-life vignette from his family helps someone you love reflect on what matters in their day and empowers them to recognize and seize the next opportunity she (or he) has to act on the right thing rather than letting it pass by unnoticed.

Today, I made a new friend.

I wasn't expecting to make a new friend.

I wasn't even looking to make a new friend.

Why don't you tell me about it?

Daddy, I was just <u>going</u> to tell you about it...

I was playing with
my friend, Maya,
on the playground
during recess.

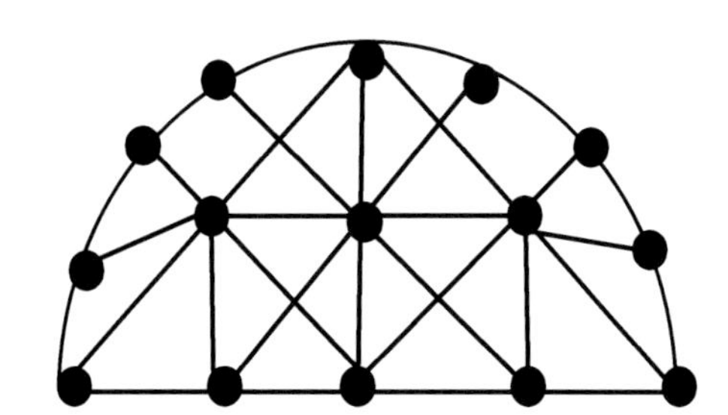

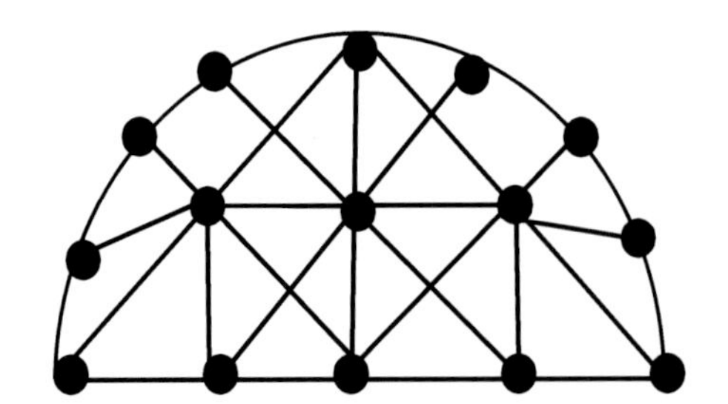

Catch the ball!

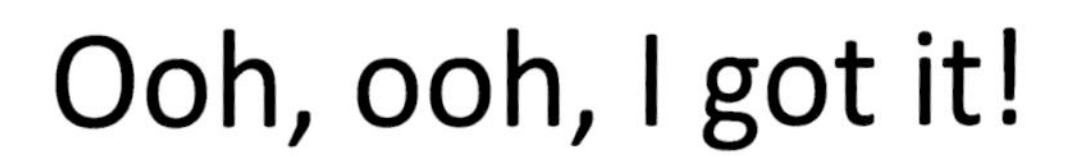

We were playing catch at first.

Good Throw!

Good catch!

Then hide and seek...

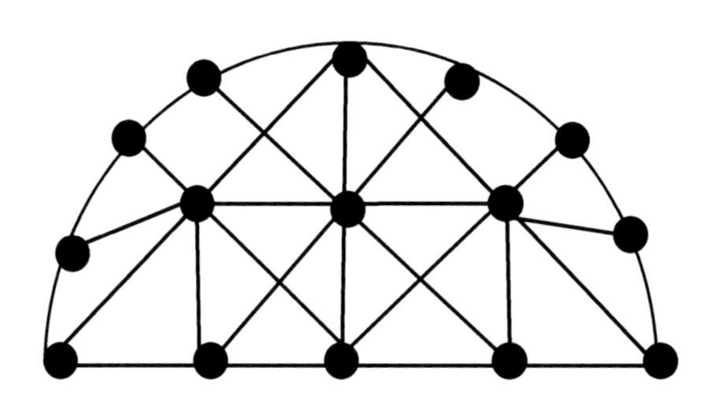

I’m super sneaky when I play hide and seek because I move hiding places when the seeker can’t see me.

Ahhhh, super sneaky hide and seek. I love it!

When Maya was peeking behind the climbing wall, I was hiding under the hanging bridge.

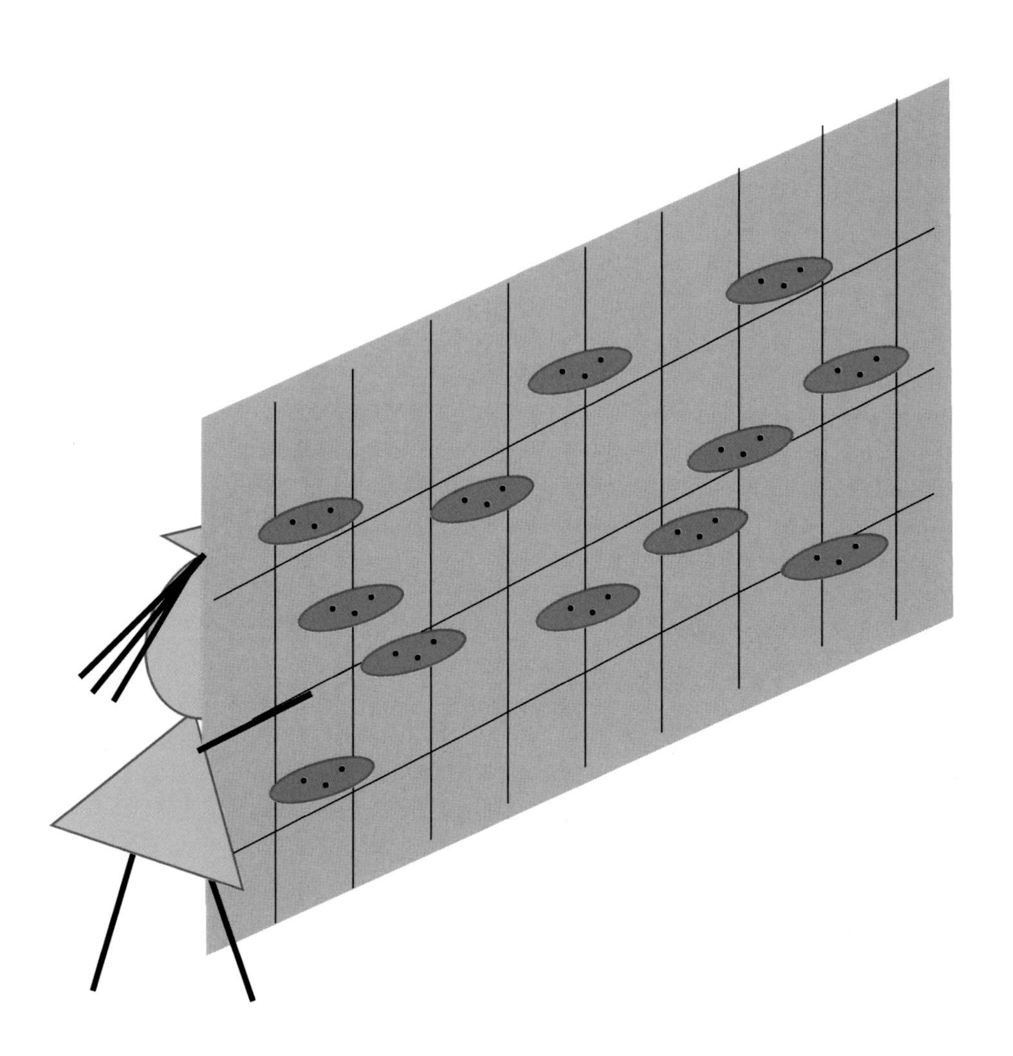

When she went to look behind the big slide, I was crouching behind the lily pads.

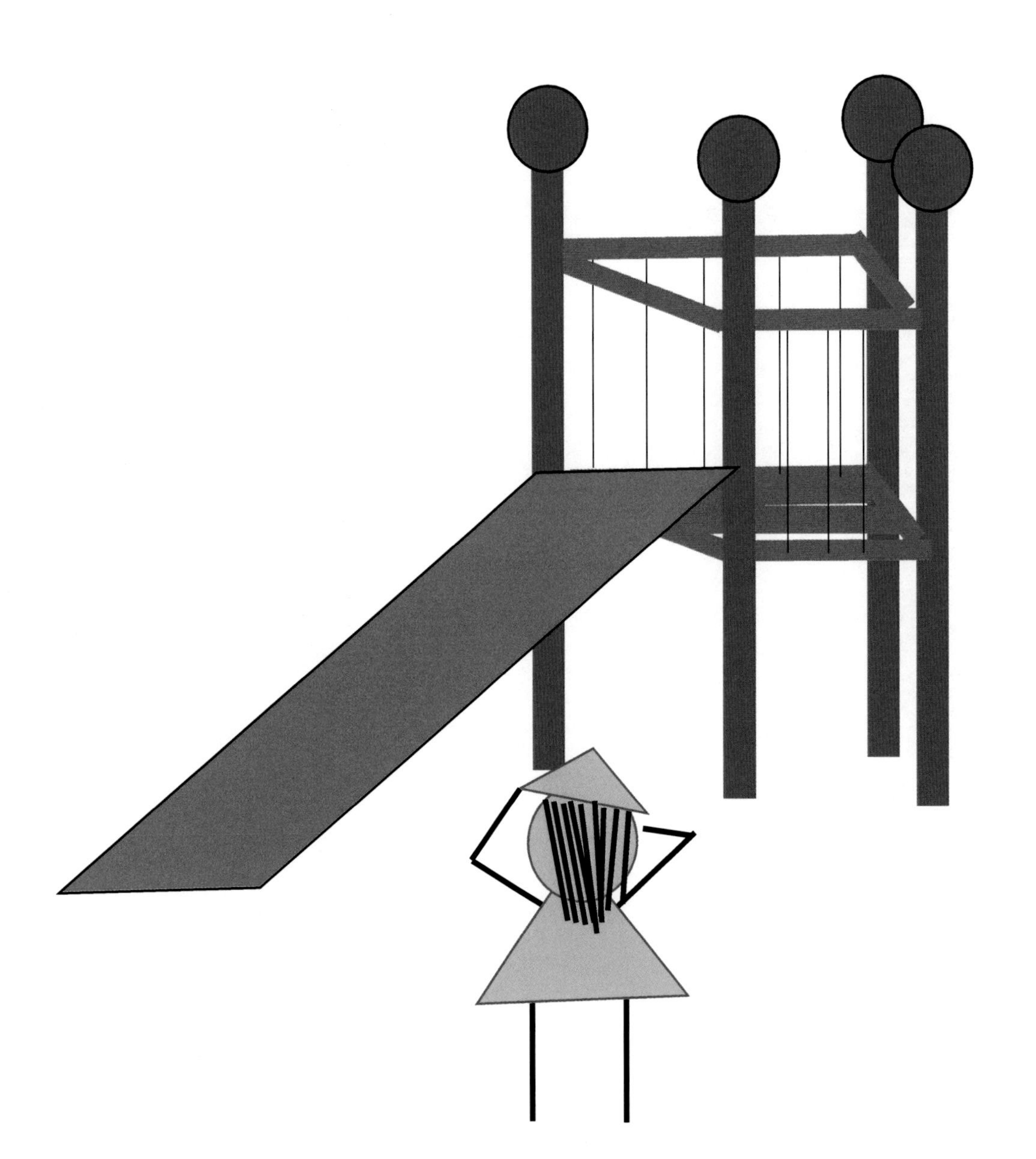

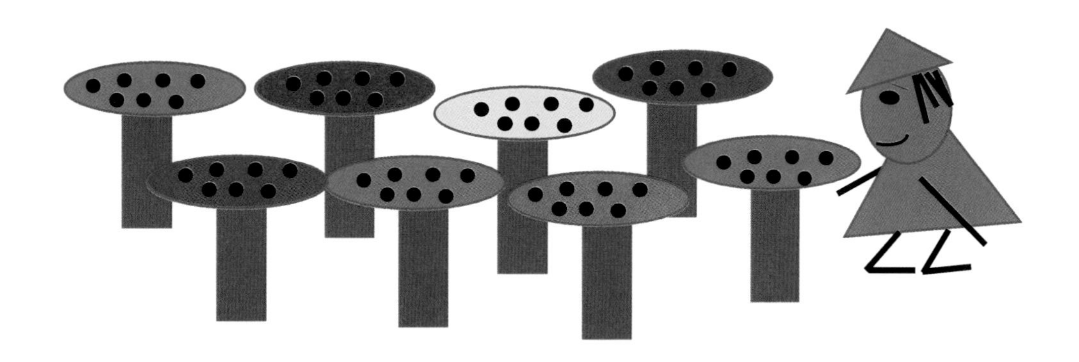

You were working hard in that game. I love it!

Anyway, when I was hiding behind the climbing wall, I saw a little girl all alone on the seesaw… and you can’t even play on the seesaw all alone.

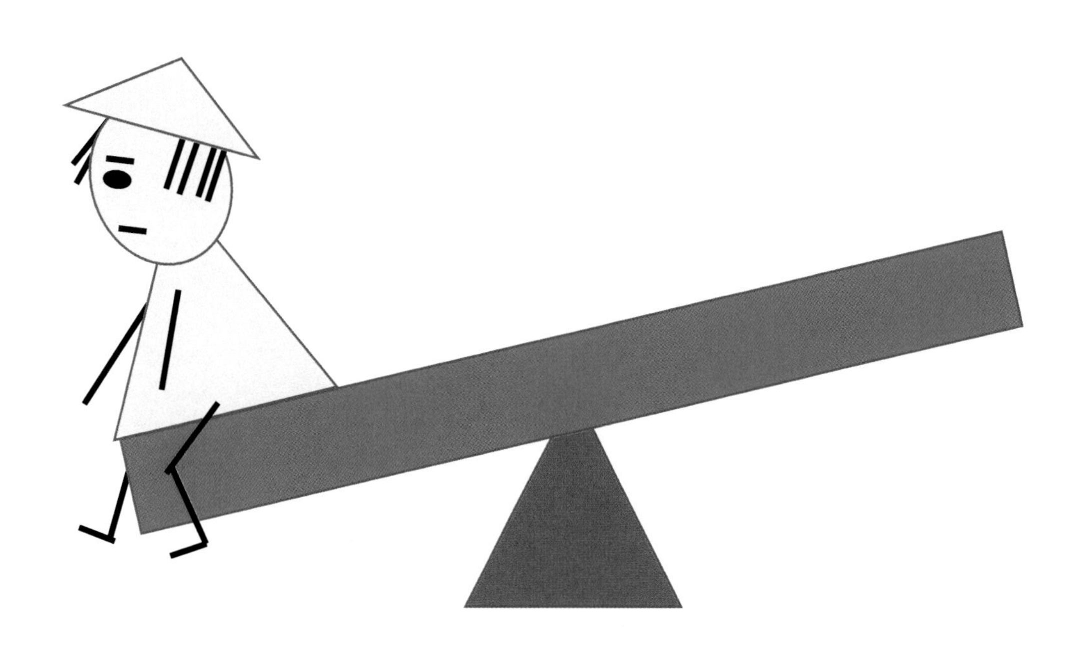

I wanted to help her, but I was busy hiding. Then...

I knew what to do!

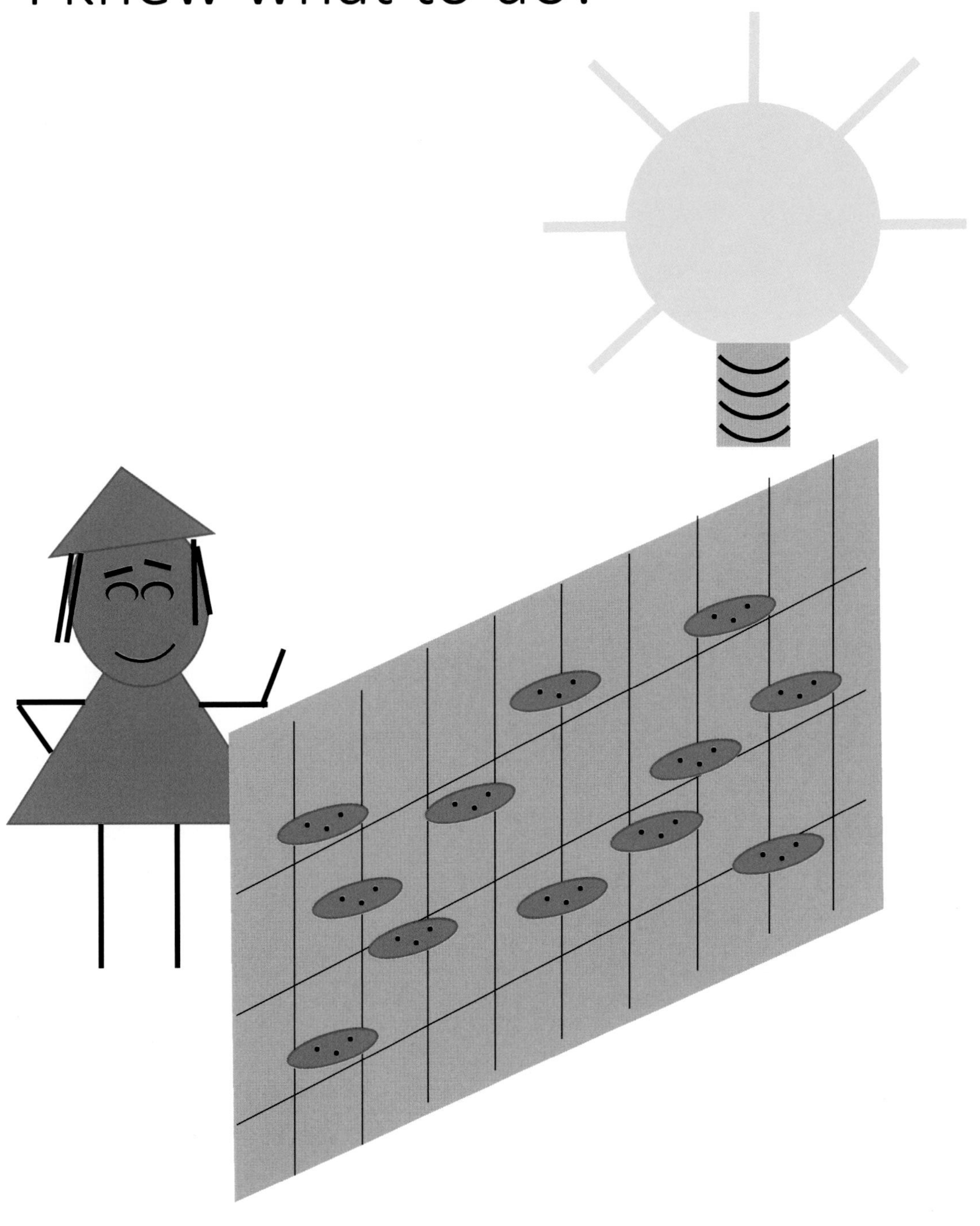

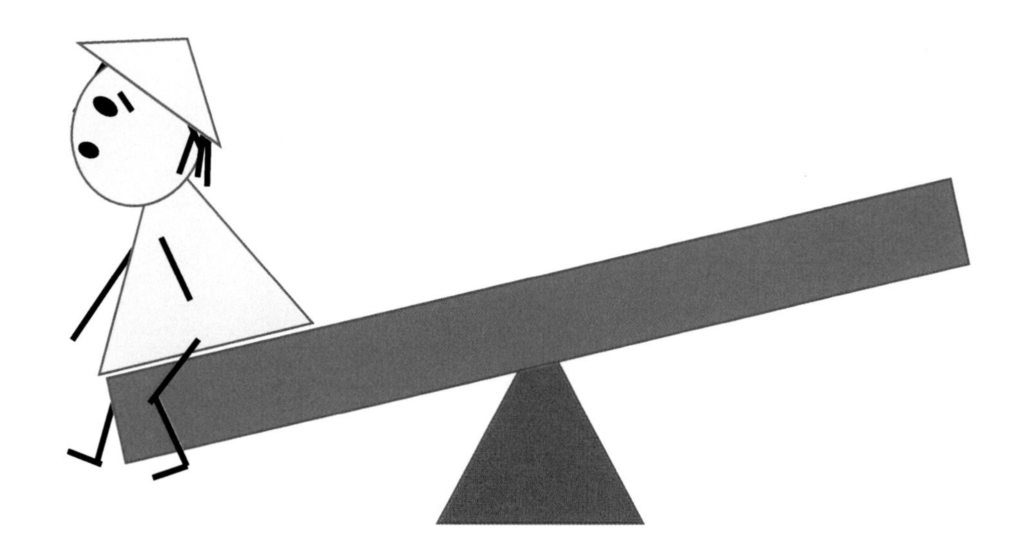

I left my hiding place and
asked her to play.

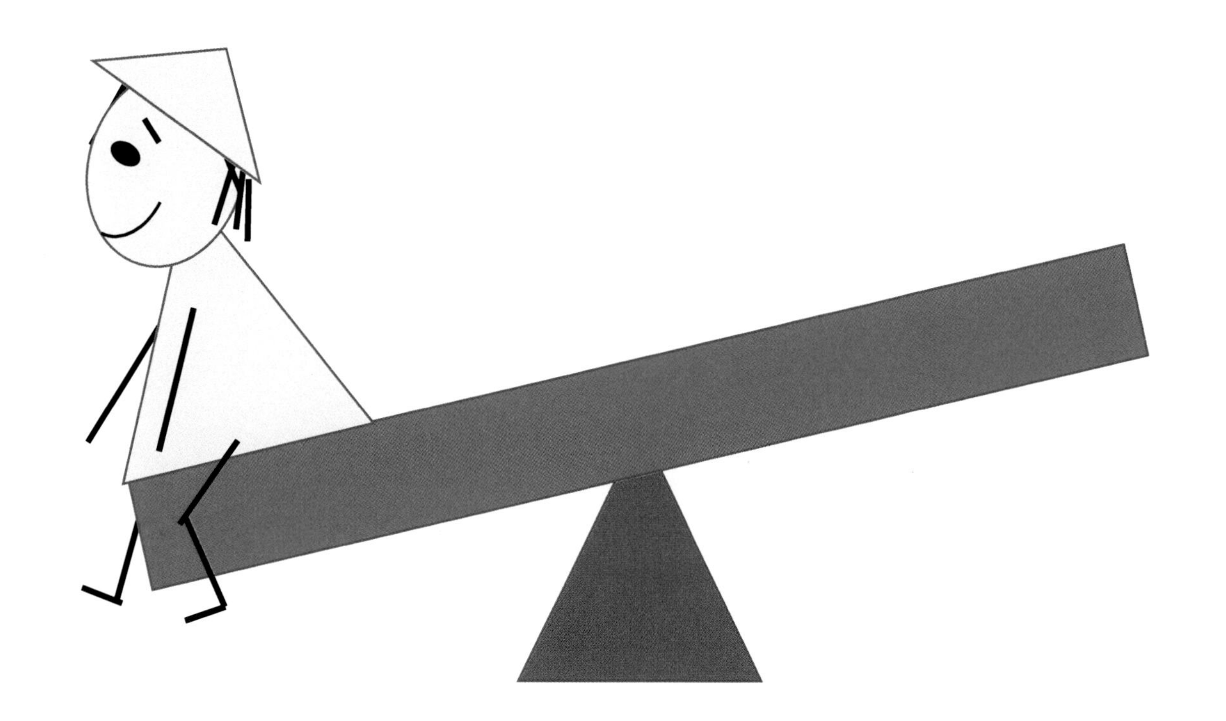

She said, “Yes!”

So we played!

Good move, that was the right thing to do.

Weren’t you worried that the seeker would find you?

Yes Daddy, I was a little worried but I did it anyway, and it didn’t even matter.

Because all three of
us played!

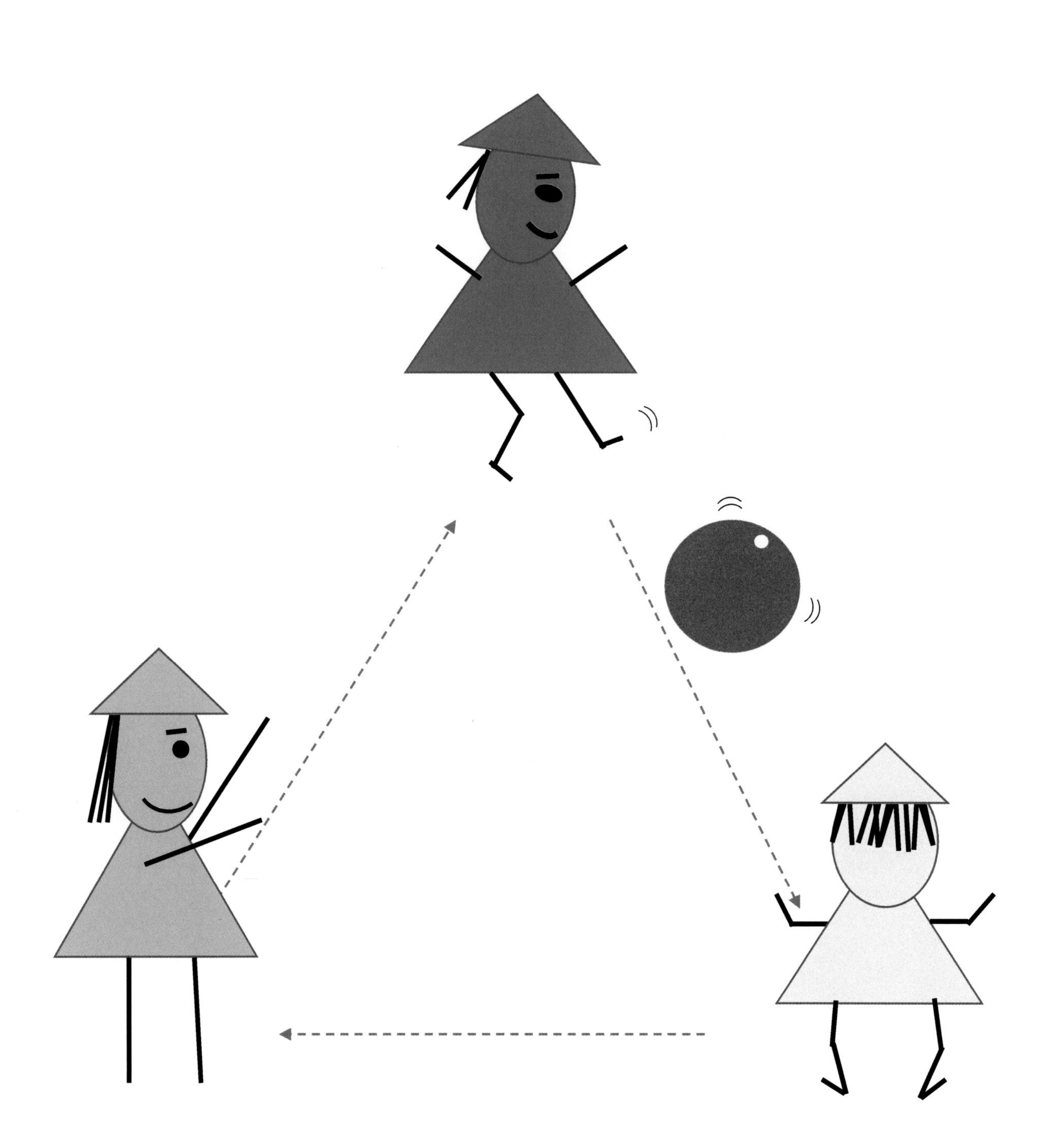

We kicked a ball in a triangle since there were three of us.

We played “Red light - Green light.”

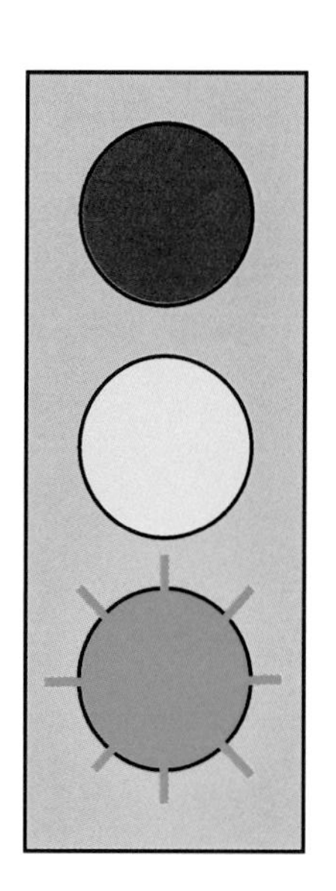

We ran so fast!

When recess was over, we had to go back to our different classrooms.

She wasn’t in our class,
but she is my friend.
I can have friends not
in my class you know.

Of course you can!
You were kind to see another girl who needed a friend!
You were brave to leave your hiding place and include her!
I’m happy that it turned out so well for all of you.
I’m so proud of you, and I love you so much!

Available titles in this series include:

Self-Discipline

Equanimity

Moral Courage

About the Author:

Jason resides in Falls Church, Virginia with his wife (an LCSW), daughter, soon to be born son, and loyal cocker spaniel.

He is an amateur historian and aspiring stoic who co-authors books with his daughter.

Together they draw on real-life childhood experience to provide practical lessons in resilience for children (and parents) in entertaining, age appropriate, ways.

His goal is that your reading experience leads to more meaningful discussion, reflection, and connection with your child.

For periodic updates and announcements on new books and events email:
littlestoics@gmail.com
with "subscribe" in the subject line.

Made in the USA
Coppell, TX
29 October 2019